Morag the Unhappy Witch

A STORY CREATED by GINO ZANI

Marfa House
Marfa, Texas

Marfa House
Marfa, Texas

MORAG THE UNHAPPY WITCH

Published by Marfa House

ISBN: 978-1-946072-10-8

DEDICATION

To my late father and my mother, my sister Maria,
my brother Paolo, my sister Daniela,
my nieces, and nephews, this book is for all of us.

Have you ever had days
where nothing goes as planned?

No matter how much you wish
they would.

Well one poor, unfortunate creature best
known to the village of MacDuff, lying at the
base of Fire Mountain, Morag McTarrget was
constantly receiving her fair share of these
unfortunate events on an infinite number of
occasions for the last few months.

Morag belonged to a well-respected ancient family of witches and warlords, who have been raised to protect and fiercely guard the village of MacDuff.

MacDuff has been a gateway between the two realms for generations. Over 1000 years to be exact. Morag fought her gift though, she had inherited it from her much revered mother Lizzie, who sadly passed away several years before, leaving Morag as the last of her kind and the last gate keeper to the two realms. Only Morag didn't ask for this, she didn't want this.

Her mother's funeral turned into a state occasion, with all the spell casters from Scotland to Uganda coming over to pay their respects to a leader who lived, dedicated, and showed such devotion to her chosen path. She was extremely loved, well respected and seen as the most powerful witch on earth.

The wake lasted three days and three nights. Everyone was drinking fermented ogre slim and eating Morag's infamous toadstool and peat bog pie. They were all jigging and giggling from sunset to sunrise, Morag preferred a cheese burger and chips with a coca cola.

Although Morag's mother is not here on earth in the physical sense, she still maintains contact with her beloved daughter through an enchanted mirror, which is a mysterious portal to the afterlife, when Morag requires counsel, converse or seeks advice from her mother.

All she needs to do is stand in front of the mirror and chant her mother's name three times and a bright swirl

of multi-coloured spark of light will appear just like a spectacular kaleidoscope pattern and then her beautiful mother's image is projected into the room.

Recently Morag has required numerous consults with her mother more than usual as her training was incomplete; she hadn't fully accepted her gifts. This was due to the distributing fact that her powers were growing and had created a series of embarrassing errors. They were simple spells that even a new-born goblin could easily do. So many would laugh at Morag's sheer stupidity.

Morag was quickly outshining the village idiot, her street cred was rapidly going down the pan. She was extremely upset with the whole sorry affair.

One more frightfully embarrassing mistake which was mockery towards the McTarrget name was when Morag was handsomely commissioned to concoct a cough mixture for Maria Vegas, the proprietor of the fashionable Tapas bar. Tapas Bar was recently opened in the village street.

MacDuff was evolving into an urban and trendy village. Gone were the traditional shops of yesterday like old Miss Tuck's sweet shop. The village council had decided to replace them all with trendy coffee spots, burger joints, bars and fashionable boutiques. It was the hip village of the Scottish highlands.

Morag handed Maria her cough medicine but she gave her a horse mixture by mistake. When Maria arrived home after a late night shift at the Tapas bar, she consumed the vile green liquid. She immediately felt strange and her body started to violently convulse. She let out a loud shriek and her husband ran to the kitchen.

She was bemused and extremely frightened at what
was befalling her, instead of a familiar scream she heard
neighing coming from her mouth. She stared at her
husband, who stood at the kitchen door in shock.

Immediately she stood on all fours. There was an open window in the kitchen, she galloped towards the open kitchen window and flew out of it. Her husband still stood there in shock. With break neck speed she galloped into the haunted forest which encloses the village, it was forbidden for mortals to enter unless you are granted a pass by the village council.

Maria now happily resides there with other horses. Her poor husband Jock is in bits. They were only married a year. He was born in MacDuff village. He went to join the navy, when he was a young boy. He met his wife Maria in Catalina, they were married there.

Morag always thought Jock and her would marry one day. She was over the moon when Jock came back. Her heart was broken when she found out he had married Maria, even though she liked Maria.

Poor Morag has been unsuccessful in removing and reversing the spell. She truly couldn't understand what went wrong with the whole process. Was it her broken heart? People started to believe that she had turned to the dark side.

A new day was dawning over the sleepy village. The golden sun was shining radiantly. Its rays were glowing and dancing along the lily-filled duck pond. The pond was just behind the local primary school.

Birds, butterflies and bees sung their numerous praises in the shelter of the local forest.

In a small wooded grove stood Morag's quaint, little, white stone built croft. And at the top of the hill was another castle that looked sort of medieval that had been deserted for years. This is where the evil Earl Macduff would torture local peasants. This is where he had turned to the dark side. There was a huge battle where Morag's family fought and won. They managed to banish the evil Earl MacDuff to the other realm. Morag stood at the gateway of the other realm. Her family had lived there for generations. Her family raised highland cows, chickens, geese, pigs, horses and they have the biggest vegetable patch in the whole county with the biggest pumpkin.

In a far corner off the newly decorated living room, a vast black cauldron was ferociously bubbling away causing its contents to splash on the wooden floor. Morag's ever faithful black cat, Magenta, busily lapped up the magical liquid. Suddenly she began to cough and vigorously shake. Large pink spots started appearing in her lovely jet black fur that reminded Morag of dark winter nights. Magenta's body slowly began to expand; it looked like a hot air balloon in pre-flight. She began to float slowly, letting out a large meow as she glided towards the ceiling.

Morag was just returning from the local village newsagent store where she had just purchased the weekly latest edition of the Witching Hour Times. The special feature this week was on the latest witches must have accessory, The VR800 a rocket- powered broomstick that went from 0 to1000 miles per hour. 'This will be most definitely be in every witches broom cupboard this summer' the magazine read. Morag didn't like using broomsticks to fly, she gets travel sick every time she uses one.

Some of the new found witches used vacuum cleaners to get themselves from point A to B. Morag tried it once but kept getting her feet tangled in the cord. She had even heard of numerous witches who had forgotten to unplug them causing serious damage.

That's why; Morag preferred her old trusted broomstick which she has had since she was a child. It was given to her by her late father, a powerful wizard. She affectionately calls it, Sticks.

She also had to buy her essential supply of newts eyes, which were becoming more scarce. She slowly opened the front door of her croft, she entered the hall and went into the lounge. She never expected to bear witness to the carnage which befell her.

Her hands flew to her face upon witnessing her beloved cat Magenta, floating above her head. She looked up and spotted the weather balloon.

"What went wrong this time?" gasped Morag.

She dropped her bags in horror and then she sprinted to the other side off the croft. She ran out of the back door, rushing into the over grown back garden, untangled the clothes line from its rusty post. Rushing back in, she immediately tied one end of the clothes line with a double

knot to the heavy cauldron's handle and the other to Magenta's tail. But suddenly Magenta began to expand further and floated out of an open window.

"Oh no!" screamed Morag as Magenta let out a loud meow.

The clothes line snapped with the over whelming strain and poor Magenta was catapulted into the open air. Morag ran to the front of the croft, only to catch a mere glimpse of a large pink shaped blimp floating away in the wide blue yonder.

"Oh, what am I going to do?" wailed Morag.

Then she noticed a familiar figure walking up her garden path.

It was Fergus, the village postman, who had served the entire county for more than 40 years. He was feeling the passage of time. He would be seventy-two soon.

He was awkwardly carrying a large brown parcel under his twig like arms. He handed Morag the parcel with a huge wheeze.

"Hello, I think this is for you love."

He handed the package over to Morag, whilst having a coughing fit.

He took a deep breath and was about to leave. But then he noticed Morag's saddened expression.

"What's up dear?"

Morag began to cry and explained about Maria and poor Magenta.

Fergus reassured her by saying, "Don't you worry, you're just having a bad spell of it. You mark my words, it will turn out alright in the end. You just need a little faith, tell

you what, why don't you have a nice relaxing bath of fresh frog's spawn and snake venom. That used to do the trick for your mother."

Fergus and her mother were good friends, he was like a father to Morag when she was growing up, after her father passed away.

"Thank you for listening Fergus, you are a good man."

On that note, she gave him a peck on the cheek and Fergus went back on his rounds with a spring in his step.

Morag placed the parcel on top of her oak kitchen table. She noticed it had a golden envelope attached to it.

She slowly detached the envelope and she opened it with her mother's letter opener. The letter inside informed her that she was in the running for the annual spell caster awards.

Her great grandfather had started the awards eighty years ago and it is still going strong. This year was actually the eighty-first ceremony. So Morag reckoned that they would pull out all the stops.

Morag always triumphed at that event since she began to participate. It was just last year she lost the prize to Matilda Higgins, her sworn enemy.

Unfortunately Morag had to give away the award to Matilda as all the previous winners are meant to do.

Morag carefully unwrapped the parcel, she liked to recycle the paper, you know do her part for the environment, she loves to do her part for the environment. She collected rain water to use for her water. She even purchased her own wind turbine to generate her own electricity.

On opening her parcel, which was addressed to her from her great Aunt Kitty, who moved from Scotland and now resided in Salem, she was so delighted to discover an elegant black velvet dress with a matching cape.

It had a small note attached which read:

> *To my special niece,*
> *Good luck in the contest. Your mother would've*
> *been proud of you. I hope you like the outfit.*
>
> *With all my love,*
> *Your Great Aunt Kitty*
> *xxxxx*

Morag ran upstairs with the dress. She immediately tried it on, it looked beautiful against her long wavy auburn hair. Her beautiful eyes, one green and one blue, her pale white skin, and red rosey cheeks with red lips, she looked amazing. It fit her perfectly, the material flowed across her body. She changed back into her regular clothes and went downstairs to practice for the contest, which was due to be held in the grand hall of the local manor. It had been moved from the village hall to accommodate the larger crowd. The contest would start in a few weeks' time, Morag was nowhere near ready.

All the spells that she tried went drastically wrong.

She accidentally added too many bats wings to the love potion which caused an explosion which almost took the croft roof off, it could be heard for miles. Several of the local villagers ran out into the streets thinking that a bomb had been detonated.

Morag became so depressed with the whole situation that she immediately got on the phone in the hallway and invited her best friend Kismet Cameron, a local spell-caster in training, over for a stop of dinner and good old fashioned chatter.

Morag got started preparing her special broth, which normally comprised of newt eyes, bats wings, nettles, and finally the rat tails, Kismet's favourite. She stirred the huge pot and carefully readjusted the seasoning by adding a dollop of frog spawn. It was just reaching eight o'clock when the silence was interrupted by a knock on the door. Morag opened the door and she was pleased to see her old friend standing on her porch, she embraced her tightly.

"I take it that you're pleased to see me." gasped Kismet, trying to get her breath back. Morag led her friend into her living room and began to sob uncontrollably.

"I'm such a failure," Morag whined as she tried to control her tears.

"No you are not." replied Kismet, who placed a reassuring arm over her friend's shoulder.

"I can't do anything right, I frequently get everything mulled up. I should be ashamed to a call myself a witch!" Morag cried as tears cascaded down her rosey coloured eyes.

"Listen, why don't we have something to eat and have a nice chat? Don't tell me you made my favourite rat tails broth." Kismet smiled.

She was so famished that she could gnaw off Maria Vegas's leg. It had been two weeks since Morag turned Maria into a wild horse.

Jock was now running the Tapas bar on his own.

Kismet and Morag moved into the kitchen.

Morag started to dish out the broth and she served it with baked bread. The broth had been taught to her many moons ago by old Granny Ferguson, who lived at the Foothills of Fire Mountain.

Kismet took a large spoonful of the broth and said, "Morag I don't know how to tell you this. The broth tastes funny. It has a certain taste of cats' tails."

"Since you mentioned it, the broth does have quite an unusual aftertaste." Morag agreed.

Kismet pondered for a while and eventually rose from the table, gradually making her way over to the kitchen cupboard and grabbed a can. She brought it back over to Morag, who moved back into the living room.

"Morag, I'm holding a can in my hand. Now please could you tell me what's written on it?"

Morag squinted her eyes and immediately exclaimed, "It's a family size tin of rat tails!"

"I don't know how to say this, but you're wrong." replied a crest fallen Kismet.

Morag blubbered, "What's wrong with me?"

"Now, I have an idea of what is going on with you." Kismet said.

"What is it? Don't keep me in suspense." Morag begged.

"I think someone in the village high street may have the answer to your prayers." teased Kismet with a wry smile on her face.

"Tell me!" shrieked Morag, who felt like her head, was going to explode with all the tension.

"Make an appointment tomorrow with Tom MacDonald, the optician." Kismet explained.

"How is he going to help me in restoring my magical powers?" scoffed Morag.

"Think about it, you get the tins muddled up and all the spells that you do seem to go wrong because you're misreading the incantations. I'm sorry to say this, but basically you're a blind bat." laughed Kismet.

"You don't have to be so blunt, but maybe you're right. It won't hurt to visit Tom in the high street for an eye test. I reckon its long overdue." replied Morag, who was now was very content with the revelation.

"It's getting late Morag. I think you better catch up on your beauty sleep. You are not getting any younger!" taunted Kismet

"You know how to make a girl feel good about herself." laughed Morag

"I aim to please." retorted Kismet.

She gave her friend a huge hug and sent her on her way.

Morag made herself a cup of hot steaming dragon milk, followed by a bath filled with soothing lavender and nettle oil. That night was the first night in months that she slept without a care in the world. She rose at the crack of dawn with a new spring in her step. Morag washed the tiredness from her eyes and brushed the cobwebs from her hair.

She came down for breakfast and cleared the mess that she had left. She had decided to go bed without clearing up. Her breakfast consisted of a bowel of cricket muesli, a huge boiled ostrich egg, which she downed with a large tumbler of serpents' blood.

After breakfast Morag decided to spruce up the house and make that important telephone call. She nervously dialled the number, it seemed to take forever for someone to answer, then suddenly,

"MacDonald Opticians, how may I help you?" responded the receptionist.

"Hello this is Ms. Morag McTarrget." She said stuttering, "I would like to make an appointment." She replied finally getting the words out.

"I don't have any appointments left for this week. I can give you a two o'clock next Thursday if that's ok with you, Ms. McTarrget." replied the soft spoken receptionist, whose calm voice made the call less stressful for Morag.

"That would be fine, thank you."

"See you then." replied the receptionist, before the line went dead.

The morning flew by, Morag got herself ready. She had decided to put her hair up and put some make-up on. She had been waiting for this appointment for over a week. It was almost half past one. Morag went downstairs to fetch her old trusted broom - stick from the cupboard under the stairs. She took her travel sickness pills; she couldn't travel anywhere without her faithful companion, Sticks.

She climbed onto her broom-stick and headed towards the village at a great velocity.

She arrived right on time and parked her broom-stick on the pavement. She placed some money in the parking meter.

She had to keep an eagle's eye out for Mary Campbell, the evil and twisted village traffic warden, who once wheel clamped a baby who was left outside a butcher shop on pram. They even say she once fined a whole funeral procession.

No one knows why she so bitter but people cross to the other side of the road to avoid her stare. There was a rumour going around town that she was half gorgon and that she could turn people to stone.

"All clear." chuckled Morag to herself.

She nervously entered the shop and nearly walked into a large display of designer sunglasses. She cautiously walked to the edge of the looming reception desk.

"Hello I'm Ms. McTarrget." croaked Morag.

"Don't be nervous, just go straight through." replied the sweet looking receptionist.

"Thank you." replied Morag who began to feel calmer. She approached the door and loudly rapped on the wooden exterior.

A meek sounding voice answered from behind the door.

"Please enter."

Morag opened the door, upon entering the darkened room she acknowledged a small, short middle-aged man sitting on a stool behind a reclining leather bound chair.

"Please make yourself comfortable." replied the man, "I don't bite."

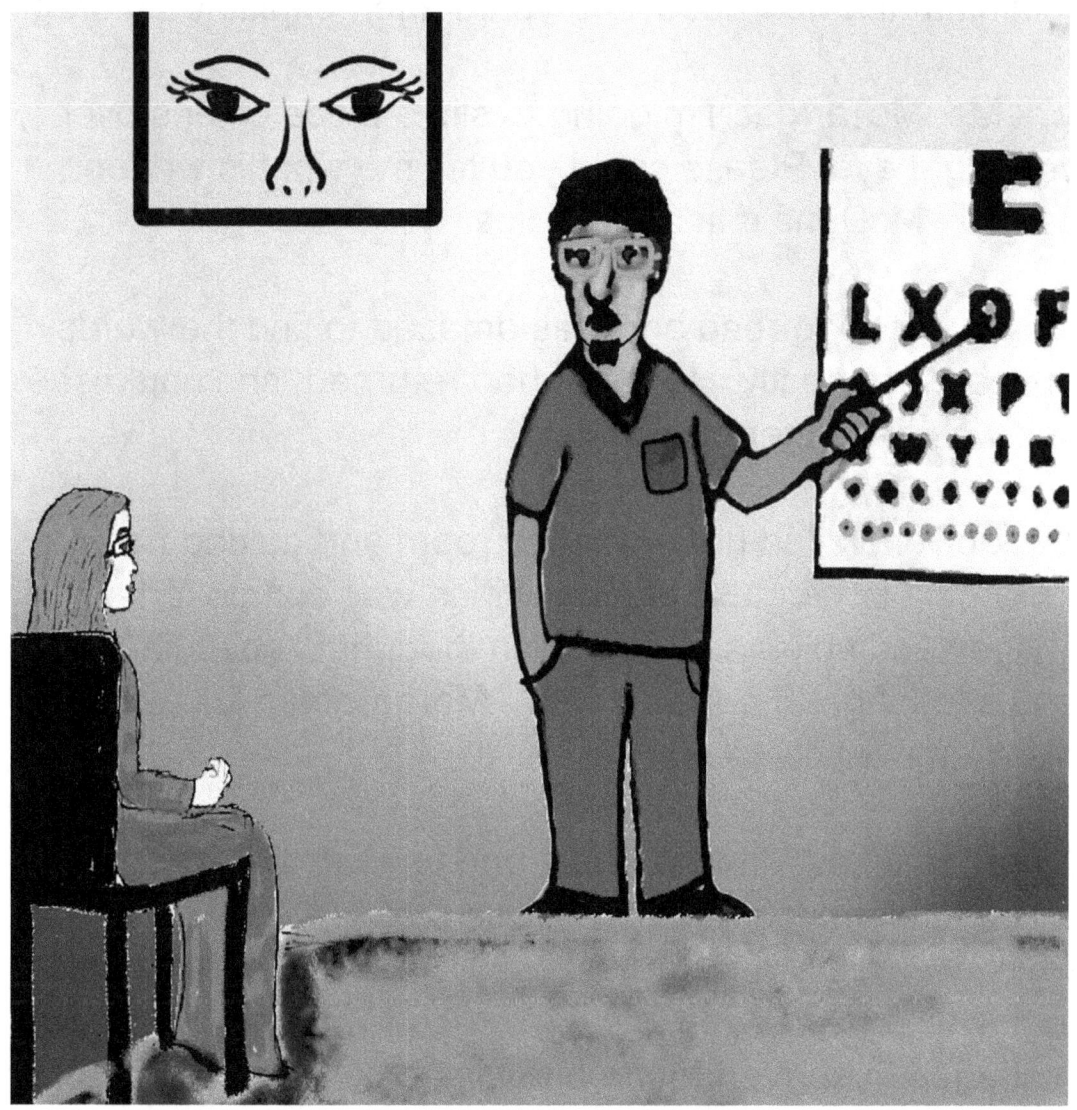

Morag eased herself into the chair and the man placed a metal contraption over both of her eyes. He then illuminated a screen, which consisted of various letters assorted in several lines.

"Please read what is written." instructed the man.

Morag started to read the letters out loud, then the man asked her when was the last time she had her eyes properly tested.

"I think that it was about two years ago." explained Morag.

"Ok Ms. McTarrget, I'm going to slip a piece of lens over your right eye. Please could you tell me what is written." said Mr. McDonald in a soft voice.

Morag began to read and was amazed to find the words appeared perfectly. Her sight had returned, she could see, she was no longer blind.

Mr. McDonald led her out of the room and guided her towards a large glass cabinet which was composed of shapes and colours. After much thoughtful speculation and a lot of great consideration, Morag opted for a pair of black rimmed glasses.

Morag thanked Mr. McDonald and flew off home to catch up on some much need regulated practice for the awards which were only a few days away. She worked from dust to dawn. She tried the love potion on two frogs. She even managed to convert Maria back, much to Jock's happiness and she turned Magenta back to normal. Morag phoned Kismet to inform her of the good news. Morag got her confidence and magic back just by wearing a pair of glasses.

The day of the awards ceremony had approached. Every witch, warlock, and wizard all over the globe were crammed like cattle into the Village Manor Hall. Morag and Kismet arrived at the venue where they unexpectedly bumped into Matilda Higgins and her horrible gaggle of old cronies.

"Look what the cat dragged in." shrieked Matilda, who had a nose like a crooked turnip, her rugged chin with wisps of hair hanging from it.

"It's Morag, the toe rag." cackled Kristy, her equally unattractive side kick. "No it's four eyes McTarrget now."

Morag just ignored them and sat down with Kismet. She had decided to dress herself in her aunt's outfit, she wore her mother's blue sapphire necklace and her hair flowed down her back. She wanted to wear it for luck.

There was a huge fanfare, everyone snapped to attention as the grand master wizard Zargo entered the grand hall and gradually made his way to the stage. He seemed to glide across the floor. People were in awe of him. He was a very intimidating figure and classily handsome according to many witches. He raised his hand in the air.

"Please be seated." Everyone sat in position.

"I welcome you all to the spell caster annual awards here at MacDuff Manor. I see that there is a great turn out this year, good luck and good spell casting." boomed Zargo, who had a voice that carried like thunder.

They all went on stage one after the other. Eventually it was Matilda's turn, much to Morag's relief she made complete and utter shambles of her whole routine. She ran off the stage wailing like a banshee.

The spotlight now fell on Morag. She slowly or rather awkwardly walked up on the stage to begin her act. There were a few hecklers in the crowd telling her to get off the stage, she blocked them out.

She commenced by making a pink elephant with blue polka dots, who was wearing a purple top hat and playing the trumpet, materialize on the stage. Everyone gasped in total amazement, even the previous hecklers were stunned into silence.

She caused a fire breathing, horn backed dragon to appear.

For the grand finale she encased the Village Manor Hall in a protected bubble and teleported it to the moon.

People got out of their seats and looked outside the windows and could see to their utter surprise the small blue globe in the distance that was earth. In a flash of brilliant light they were teleported back down to the Village Manor Hall.

Everyone in the hall gave Morag a standing ovation. She was clearly the best of bad lots. All the witches looked at her in total awe. They had new respect and admiration for her.

After the final performances the judges retired to the voting chamber for what seemed like an eternity. Later the judges returned and announced their verdict. An eerie silence went through the room, you could hear a pin drop.

Zargo dramatically strolled to the middle of the imposing stage.

He boomed, "We the judges are very pleased and honoured to announce that this year's winner is none other than Morag McTarrget!"

Everyone in the hall exploded with claps, standing ovations, whistles, and cheers. Even Matilda and that horrible hog of Kristy gave her a hug.

She eventually reached the podium where she weakly accepted her award. Morag's status had returned and everyone came across the world to visit her.

Zargo proposed to Morag a few weeks after the ceremony.

When they got married it was a huge state affair, they decided that they would get married in the local village church.

They had two children Tubby and Zargo Jnr.

So please remember dear children to get your eyes tested and perhaps you will find your own magical power.

Until the next adventure of Morag, be good!

ABOUT THE AUTHOR

Gino was very sick as a child. During his long stays in hospital he started to write and read stories to the other sick children. His family took him to a very special place close to his heart. That was Loch Lomond and Highlands. He has never been to The Island of Skye but one day he would like to visit Skye and the enchanted Island of Iona. That is where the inspiration for Morag the Witch came about.